Mr Bear's New Baby

Debi Gliori

ORCHARD BOOKS

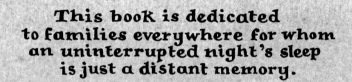

This book is dedicated
to families everywhere for whom
an uninterrupted night's sleep
is just a distant memory.

ORCHARD BOOKS
96 Leonard Street, London EC2A 4RH
Orchard Books Australia
14 Mars Road, Lane Cove, NSW 2066
First published in Great Britain 1999
© Debi Gliori 1999
The right of Debi Gliori to be identified as the Author
of this work has been asserted by her in accordance
with the Copyright, Designs and Patents Act, 1988.
A CIP catalogue record for this book is available
from the British Library.
1 86039 409 4
Printed in Belgiun

It is way past bedtime in the forest.
It is time for everyone to be asleep.
A dark and quiet time for hush and lullabies.

But lights are on at Mr Bear's house.
And listen...drifting out over the trees
is the most awful din.
It's the sound of Mr Bear's new baby
waking up.
"Oh dear," sighed Mrs Bear.
"Oh dear, oh dear," groaned Mr Bear.
"Waaaa," squeaked the new baby.

"What that baby needs is to be tucked in by her Daddy," said Mr Bear.

He climbed out of bed and went to tuck in the new baby.

But the baby squeaked more loudly. Mr Bear gazed lovingly at the baby.

"What that baby needs is some milk from her Mummy," said Mr Bear.

And Mrs Bear climbed out of the bed and fed the new baby.

But the new baby spluttered and choked and squeaked some more.

Mr Bear paced up and down, patting the new baby's back. But the new baby closed her eyes, threw back her head and opened her mouth for a huge squeak.

"Goodness," said Mr Bear, "what an enormous mouth for one so small. What you need is a lullaby." Mr and Mrs Bear sang the new baby a lullaby. But that didn't work either.

There was a knock at the door.
In staggered Mr Bun with a rocking cradle.

"Try this," he said, yawning. "When our six babies were small, this used to put them to sleep."

So Mr Bear tucked his new baby in the cradle and they all took turns rocking her.

But the cradle was too wobbly, and the new baby still squeaked.

There was another knock on the door.
In came Mrs Hoot-Toowit with a huge nest.
"I don't know if this will work for new
baby bears," she said. "But when
Little Howl was a baby, I would put her
in it, and she would fall asleep at once."

So Mr Bear lifted the new baby out of
the rocking cradle and put her in the nest.
But the nest was too prickly and the new
baby continued to squeak.

"Heavens," said Mr Bear, feeling
pretty close to squeaking himself,
"how can someone so small
make so much noise?"

One by one, all Mr Bear's sleepless neighbours
came calling with things to help the new baby sleep.

Mr Rivet-Frogge brought
his children's favourite lily-pad.
But that was too wet.

Mrs Buzz brought her infant's hive.
But that was too sticky.

Even Mrs Grizzle-Bear brought
Baby Grizzle-Bear's shawl.
But that was too woolly.

While Mrs Grizzle-Bear poured tea and Mrs Bear passed cake around, Mr Bear paced up and down with the sobbing baby over his shoulder.

"Little one," he said. "My legs are tired with all this walking."

The baby kept on crying.

Mr Bear patted the baby gently on her back and whispered in her ear. "Baby bear," he said. "My shoulder is soggy with all these tears."

The baby cried all the more.

"Good grief," said Mr Bear, feeling tired, soggy and very fed up. "What on earth can I do to stop you crying?"

A little figure appeared at the door,
trailing a blanket behind her.

"What ever are you doing up?" said Mrs Bear.

"I can't sleep," said Small Bear. "That baby
woke me up."

"You're too small to be up this late,"
groaned Mrs Bear. "Come on, back to bed."

"She's even smaller than I am," said Small Bear.
"And she's up."

The new baby looked up with a woebegone
little hiccup.

"I'm much bigger than both of you," sighed
Mr Bear, "and all I want is not to be up."

"We'd better be going home to bed,"
said Mr Bun and Mrs Hoot-Toowit.
   "Goodnight all," croaked Mr Rivet-Frogge.
   "Sleep well," added Mrs Buzz.
   "I'll come back for the shawl in the
morning," said Mrs Grizzle-Bear.

All Mr Bear's neighbours tiptoed
out leaving Mr and Mrs Bear
with their wakeful little bears.
The new baby was
still crying.

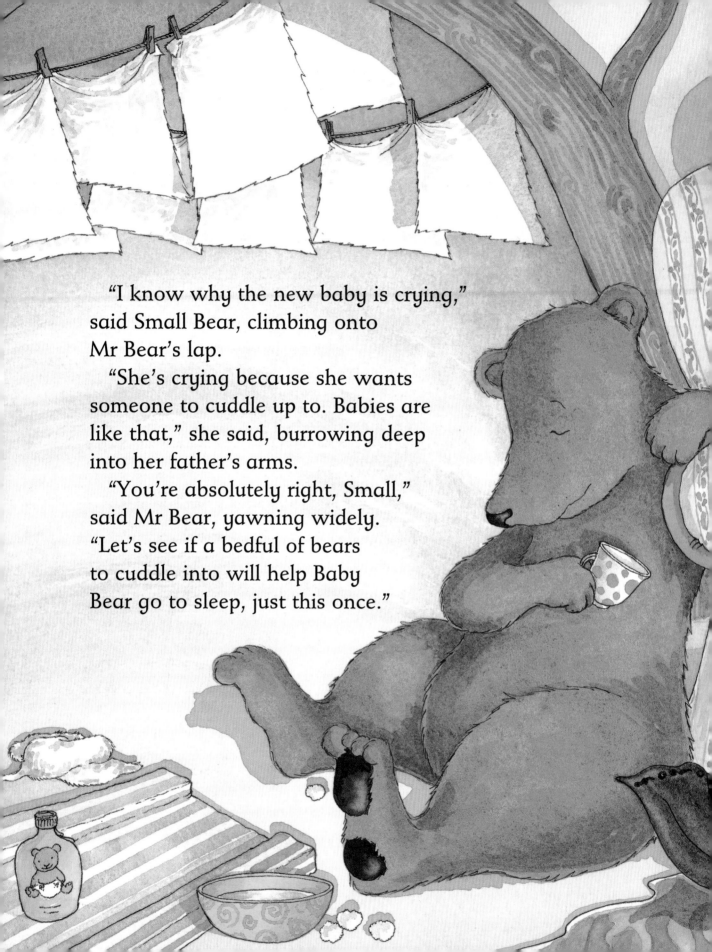

"I know why the new baby is crying," said Small Bear, climbing onto Mr Bear's lap.

"She's crying because she wants someone to cuddle up to. Babies are like that," she said, burrowing deep into her father's arms.

"You're absolutely right, Small," said Mr Bear, yawning widely. "Let's see if a bedful of bears to cuddle into will help Baby Bear go to sleep, just this once."

Carrying their little bears,
Mr and Mrs Bear climbed
upstairs to bed.

Mr and Mrs Bear's bed wasn't wobbly or prickly.
Nor was it wet, sticky or woolly.
In fact it was utter bliss…
The new baby stopped crying immediately,
gazed into Mr Bear's eyes, patted his nose and
fell fast asleep.

"My goodness," said Mr Bear, stunned by the
sudden silence.

"Well done, Small," said Mrs Bear, turning over
and starting to snore almost at once.

But Small Bear was fast asleep and dreaming
of being big and very soon, all was quiet and still.

The house was full of the sound of sleeping bears.
All, that is, except for Mr Bear.

He lay, in the dark, listening to Mrs Bear
snoring, and far off in the trees,
the sound of Mrs Hoot-Toowit
singing lullabies.
The baby stretched like a
furry starfish and smiled
in her sleep.
"How can someone so
small take up so much
room?" thought Mr Bear.

The last thing he heard before he
fell asleep was Mrs Hoot-Toowit's,
"Goodnight, goodnight to you, to you."